Thanks to Hannah—the princess up the street—
Ken Sanders Rare Books, and my mom.

Princess Wannabe
Copyright © 2014 by Leslie Lammle
All rights reserved. Manufactured in China.
No part of this book may be used or reproduced in any manner whatsoever without
written permission except in the case of brief quotations embodied in critical articles
and reviews. For information address HarperCollins Children's Books, a division
of HarperCollins Publishers, 10 East 53rd Street, New York, NY 10022.
www.harpercollinschildrens.com

Library of Congress Cataloging-in-Publication Data
Lammle, Leslie, author, illustrator.
Princess wannabe / Leslie Lammle. — First edition.
pages cm
Summary: After magically entering her bedtime fairy tale book, Fern discovers what it is like to be a princess.
ISBN 978-0-06-125197-9 (hardcover bdgs) — ISBN 978-0-06-125198-6 (lb bdgs)
[1. Princesses—Fiction. 2. Books and reading—Fiction. 3. Characters in literature—Fiction.] I. Title.
PZ7.L1819Pr 2014   2012050673
[E]—dc23   CIP
                                                                              AC

The artist used watercolor, Dr. Ph. Martin's acrylic, and pencil on American
Master's printmaking paper to create the illustrations for this book.
Title design by Iskra Johnson
Typography by Rachel Zegar
14 15 16 17 18 SCP 10 9 8 7 6 5 4 3 2 1

First Edition

Princess Wannabe

Written and illustrated by

Leslie Lammle

"Is it story time yet?"

HARPER
An Imprint of HarperCollinsPublishers

"Oops!" said the babysitter. "It is *way* past story time. Go brush your teeth while I put the baby to bed."

"But...," said Fern.

"Hurry!" said the babysitter, disappearing down the hall. "Besides, you picked another princess story— those all end the same way."

I prefer to find out for myself, thought Fern, and she opened the book.

"Ah...ahh...achoo!"
Fern brushed some dust off
the page, and her nose began to
twitch. "I want...I want...
AHhhhCHooo!
I want to know what it is like to be a
princess. If I were a princess, I bet
my wishes would always come true."
Just then, the corner of the page fluttered open. The
moment Fern turned it, she was deep inside the book.

"Oh! Lucky me—a fairy godmother!" said Fern.
"Please, oh please, would you grant my wish?"
"Sorry, dearie, not at this hour. I'm off duty.
Besides, my hands are full fixing this leak."

The fairy godmother leaned out the door.
"Perhaps a visit with the princess will help.
Just stay on the path. It leads to her castle."

Fern skipped down the hill.

She hadn't gone far when she came upon a frog smacking his lips.
He stopped and wiped the froth from his mouth.

Fern cringed. "Mr. Frog Prince, I know how your story goes.
Just because I want to be a princess doesn't mean I need a prince.
Can you keep those lips to yourself?"

"Don't fret, my lady," he said through a mouthful of toothpaste.
"I'm done kissing for the day. In fact, I am getting ready to go."
He gulped some water and returned to brushing.
Phew! Fern raced down the path.

Soon she came upon a wolf hunkered over a stump,
his claws hovering and ready to . . .

"Stop!" Fern stamped her foot. "What are you doing?
If I were a princess, I would outlaw such bad behavior."

"Good grief!" whispered the wolf. "Keep it down. Bad behavior is just my day job. Right now, I'm pigsitting for some friends. I don't want you waking the little ones. Now shoo!"

"Oh . . . er, pardon me," said Fern.

And off she ran. . . .

She stopped when the path forked. "I'm lost!" She coughed.
"And something stinks! Which way should I go?"

Fern climbed up into the treetops.
"Excuse me, Giant. Which way is the castle?"
The giant spat out his whistle and bellowed,
"Fe fi fo fum! Open your eyes, girl. Follow my thumb!"
Fern scampered down the tree . . .

...through the forest, up to the castle gate.

She stood panting
in front of a guard.
He rolled his eyes
and said, "Not another
one—you wannabe
princesses are all
the same."

"I just want to ask Her Highness—"
"The gate is closing," he interrupted. "Her
Highness has no time for you or your questions."
He pounded his lance into the ground when all of a sudden . . .

. . . the guard shrieked, "Mice! Yikes!"

"I prefer," said Fern, "to ask her myself, thank you."

And she ran into the courtyard and wandered
down halls, past miles and miles of locked doors.

She found herself in a grand hall, exhausted, staring
at a portrait of the princess. "Is this the closest I will get?"
"Eeep!"
Fern turned just in time to notice some mice scuttle
under a curtain. She ran after them.

Fern pulled the curtain back and heard an announcement:
"STORY TIME. QUIET, PLEASE."

She stared at the reader and gasped. "That looks just like..."
Speechless, she found a good place to sit and listen.

When the story ended,
Fern waited in line to say good-bye.
"Excuse me. I have one question: What is it really
like to be a princess?"
"Well," the princess sighed. "All day long I am fussed over—
cheeks pinched, collars starched, hair teased—and, worst of all,
reminded to sit up straight. If I had my wish, I would spend
my whole day relaxing with friends and a good book."
Fern thought of her comfy chair
and her pile of books and
her animal friends.

She could hardly believe the princess wished for something Fern already had. "Your Highness," Fern asked, "which is the quickest way home?"

"Oh! We specialize in shortcuts," said the princess, and she snapped her fingers and ordered some fairy dust.

Fern climbed into bed, just in time
for the babysitter to tuck her in.

The babysitter's nose twitched as
she lifted the book from Fern's arms.
"Ah…ahh…AHHCHooo!
Fern! Where did all this dust come from?"

Too tired to answer, Fern closed her eyes
and thought, She can find out for herself.